OLD DEVIL
WIND

Bill Martin Jr

OLD DEVIL WIND

ILLUSTRATED BY
Barry Root

Voyager Books
Harcourt Brace & Company

SAN DIEGO   NEW YORK   LONDON

Requests for permission to make copies of any part of the work
should be mailed to: Permissions Department,
Harcourt Brace & Company,
6277 Sea Harbor Drive,
Orlando, Florida 32887-6777.

First Voyager Books edition 1996
Voyager Books is a registered trademark of
Harcourt Brace & Company.

Library of Congress Cataloging-in-Publication Data
Martin, Bill, 1916–
Old devil Wind/by Bill Martin Jr;
illustrated by Barry Root.
— 1st ed.
p.   cm.
Summary: On a dark and stormy night one object after another
joins in making eerie noises in an old house.
ISBN 0-15-257768-8
ISBN 0-15-201384-9 (pbk.)
[1. Ghosts — Fiction.]   I. Root, Barry, ill.   II. Title.
[PZ7.M364301   1993]
[E] — dc20   92-37908

C E F D

Printed in Singapore

The illustrations in this book were done in watercolor and
gouache on D'Arches 140-lb. hot-press watercolor paper.
The display type was set in Kennerly Bold Italic.
The text type was set in Kennerly.
Composition by Thompson Type, San Diego, California
Color separations by Bright Arts, Ltd., Singapore
Printed and bound by Tien Wah Press, Singapore
Production supervision by Warren Wallerstein and Stan Redfern
Designed by Michael Farmer

To Herb Parker Jr and all the gals
— B. M.

To Kent Bulcken and Eric Phillips — "the guys"
— B. R.

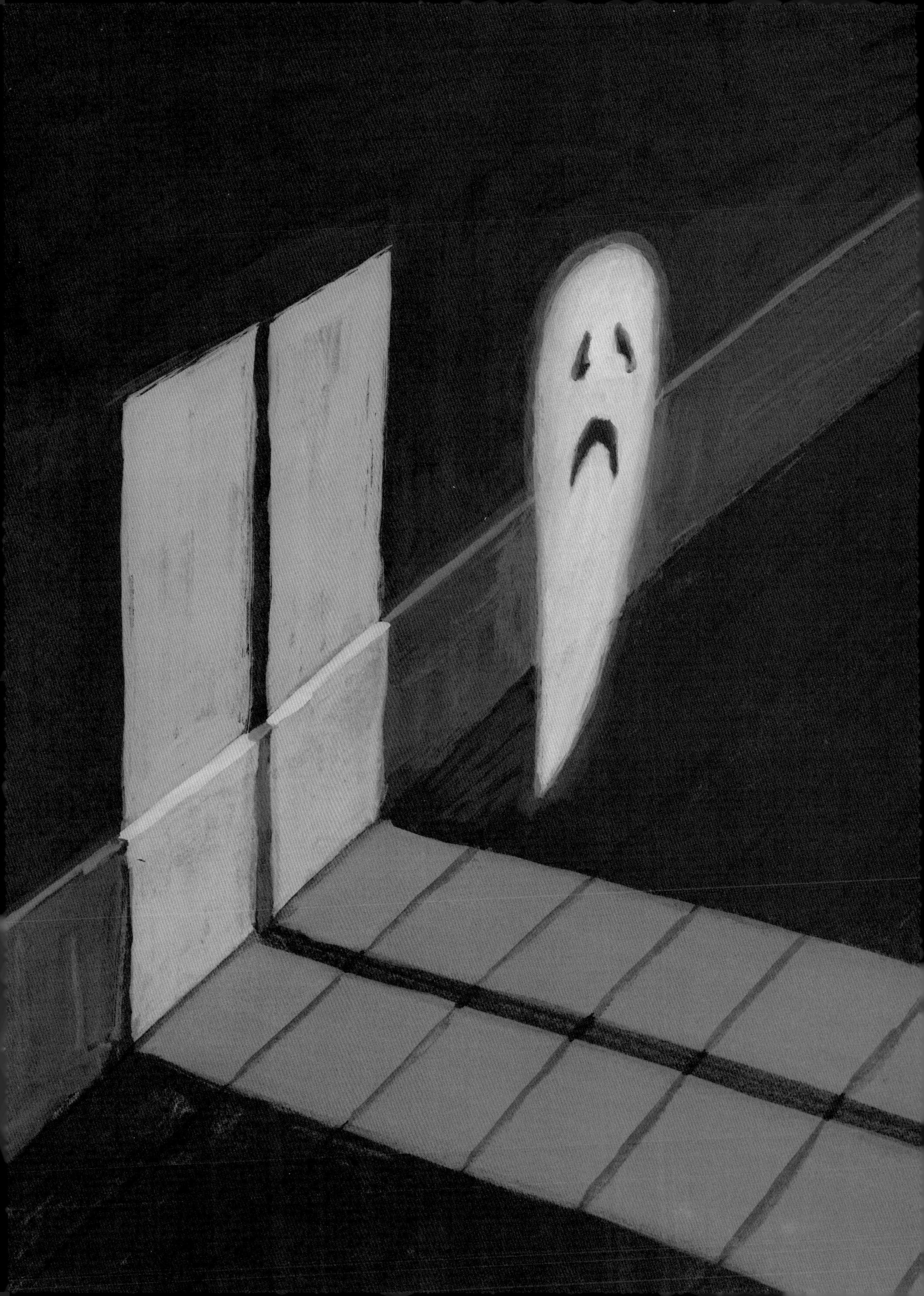

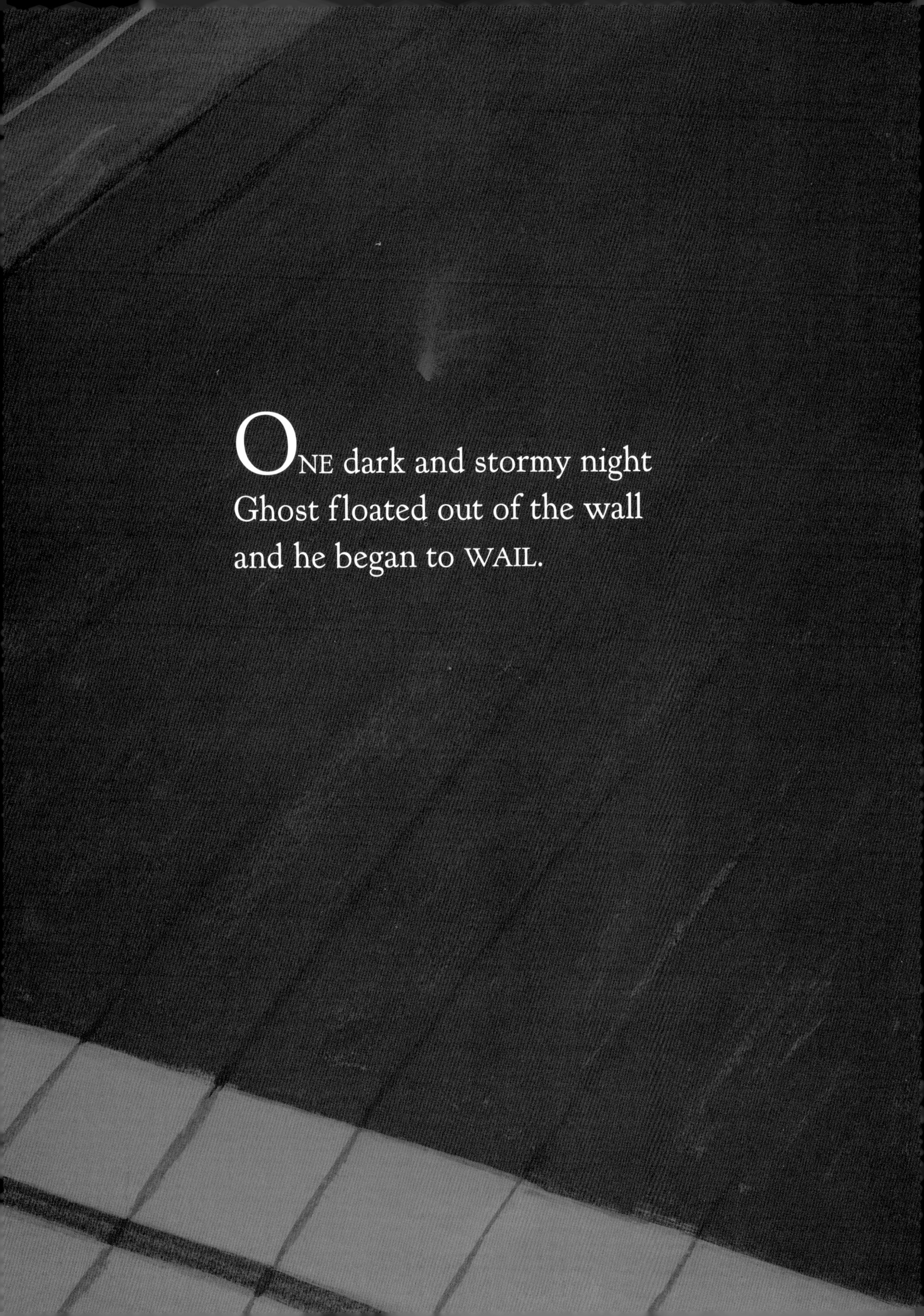

ONE dark and stormy night
Ghost floated out of the wall
and he began to WAIL.

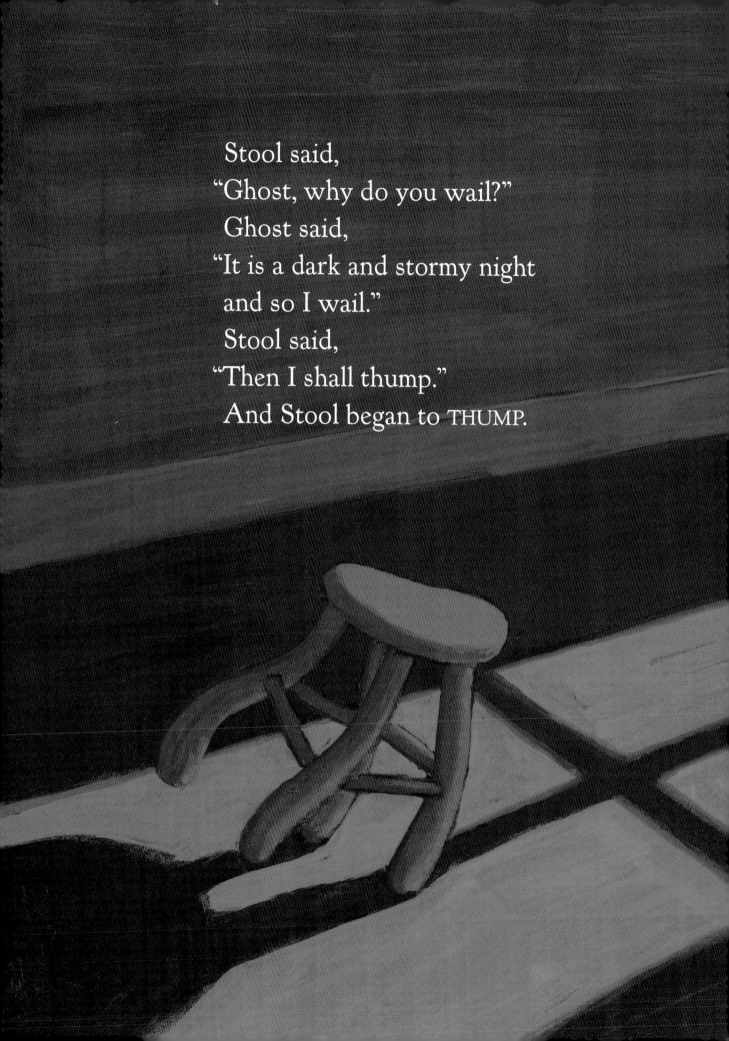

Stool said,
"Ghost, why do you wail?"
Ghost said,
"It is a dark and stormy night
and so I wail."
Stool said,
"Then I shall thump."
And Stool began to THUMP.

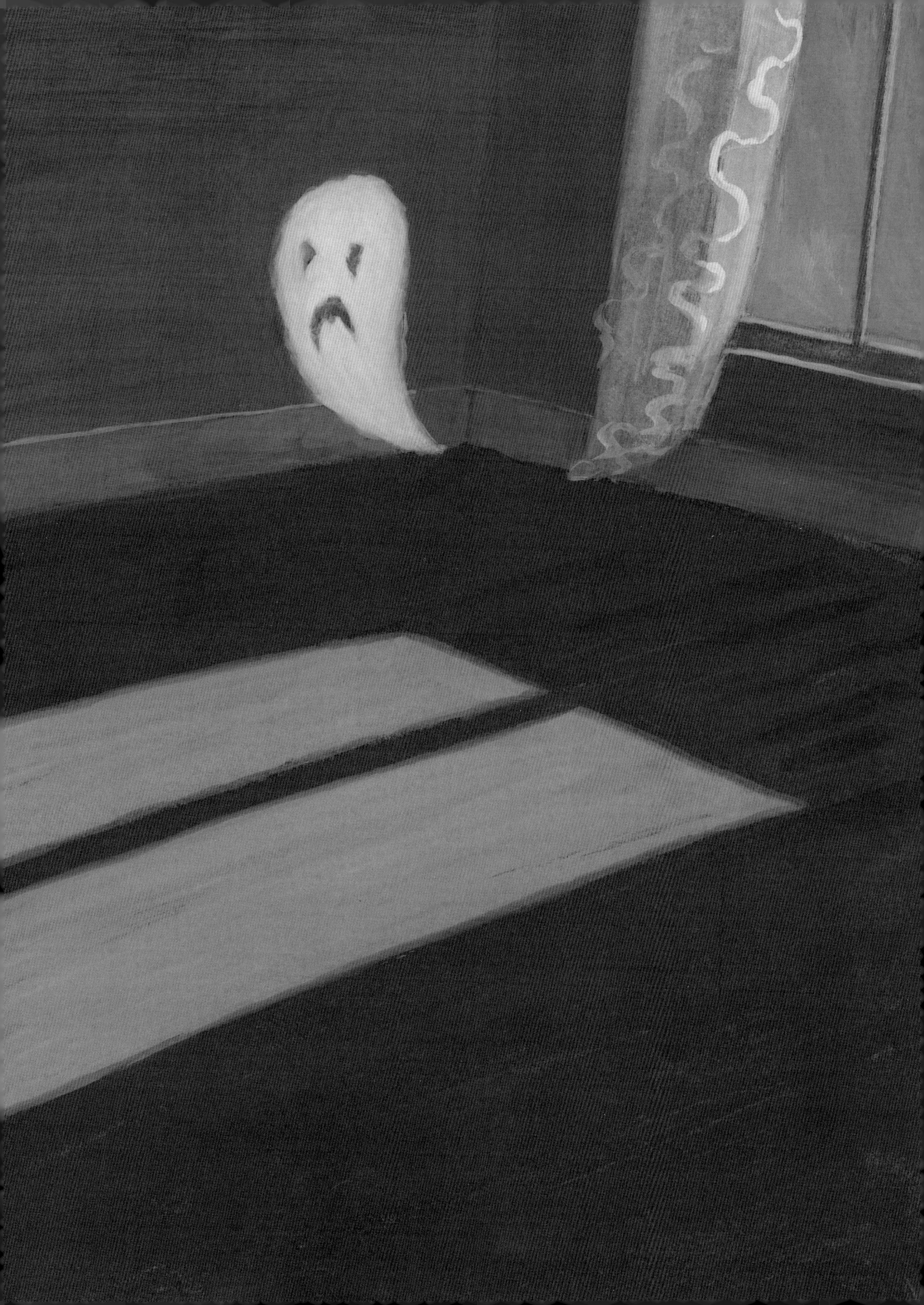

Broom said,
"Stool, why do you thump?"
Stool said,
"It is a dark and stormy night.
Ghost wails
and so I thump."
Broom said,
"Then I shall swish."
And Broom began to SWISH.

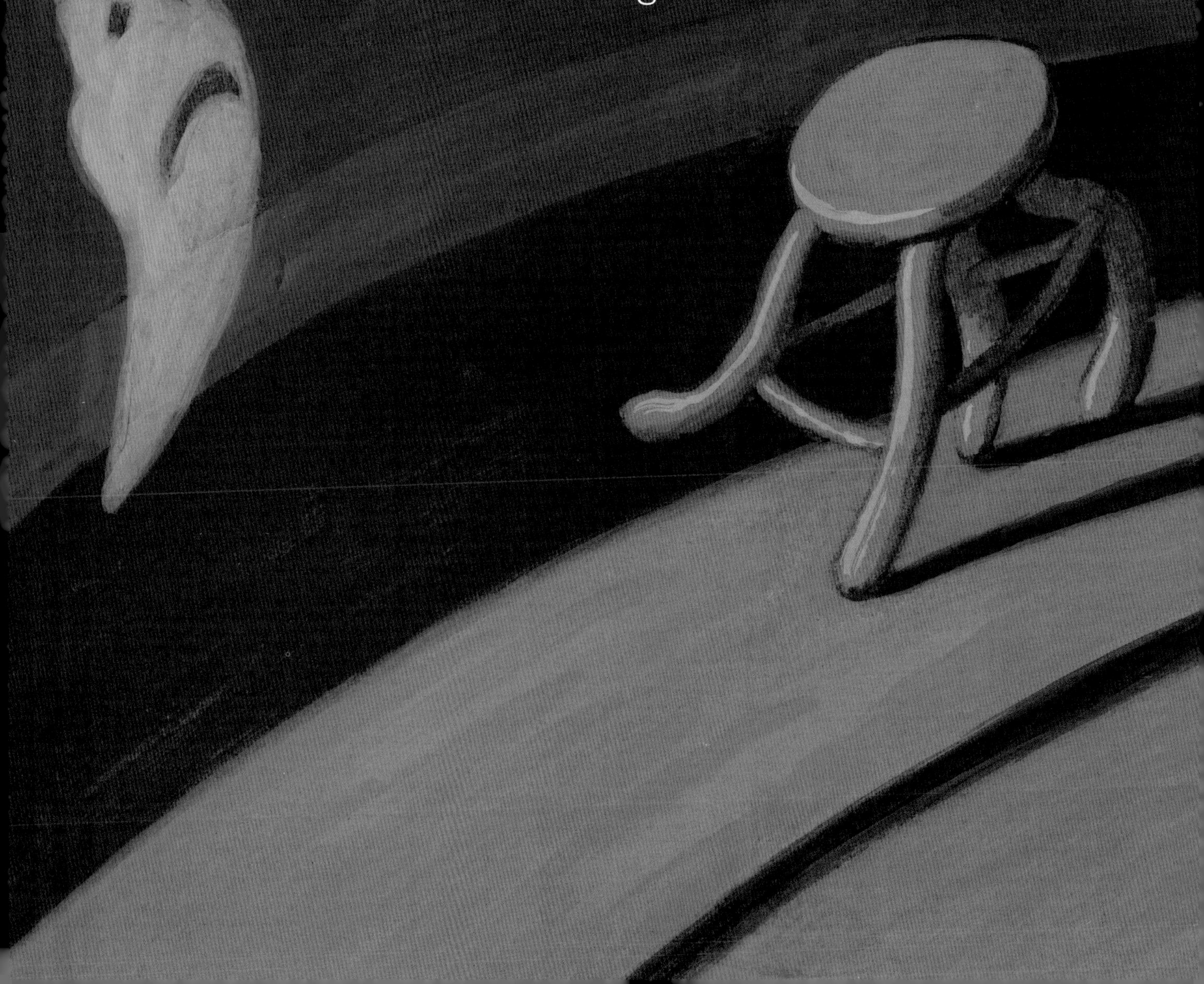

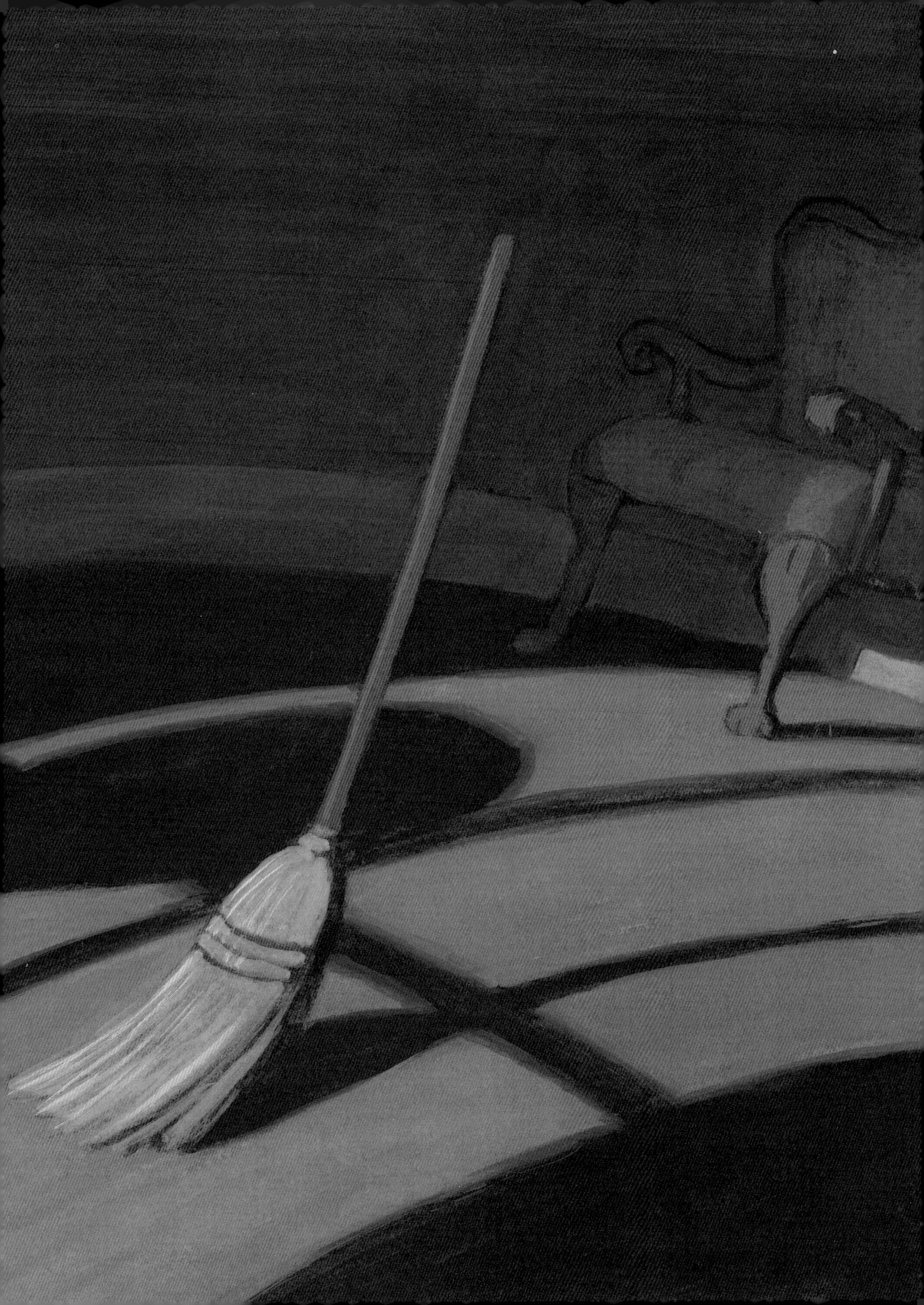

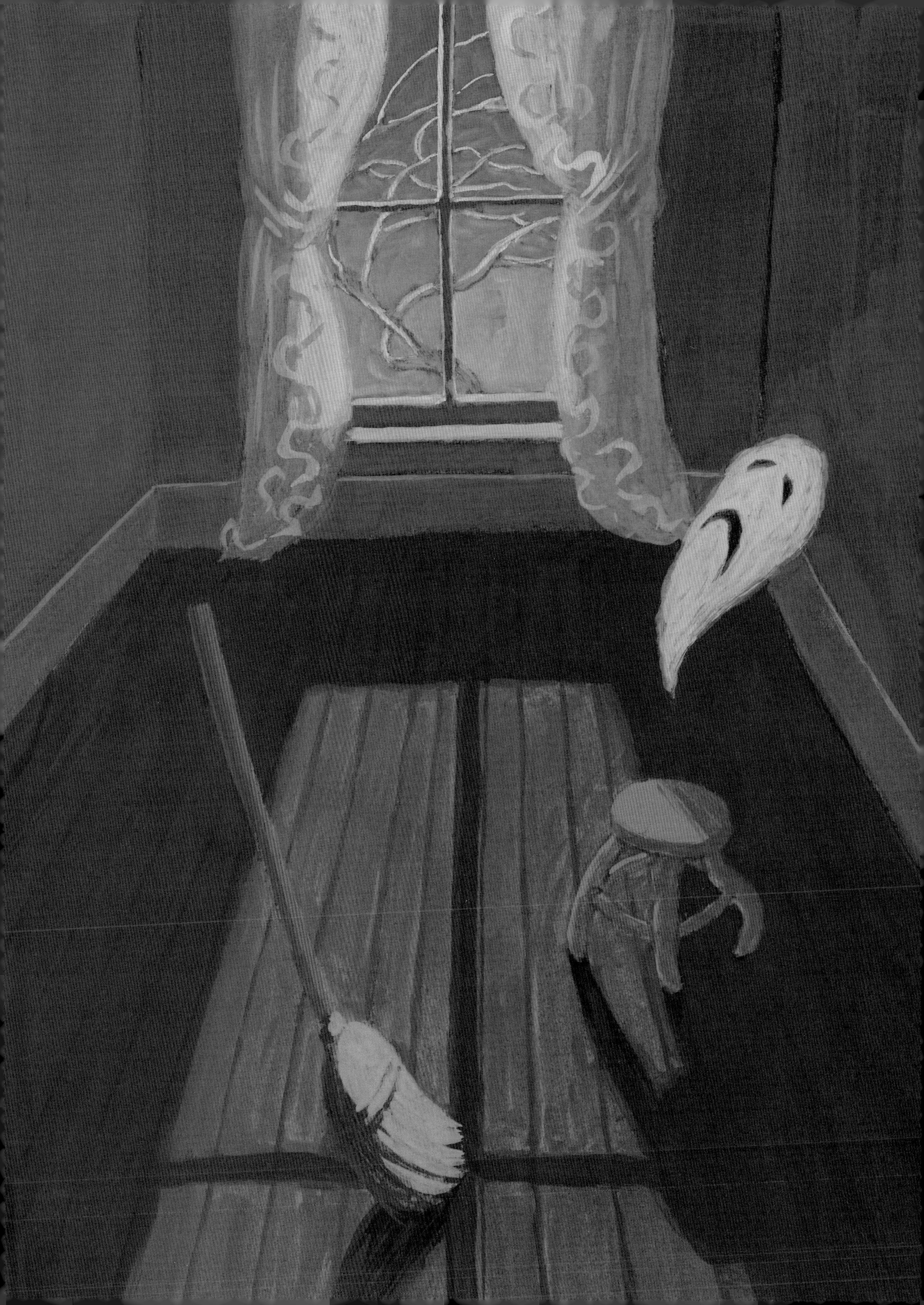

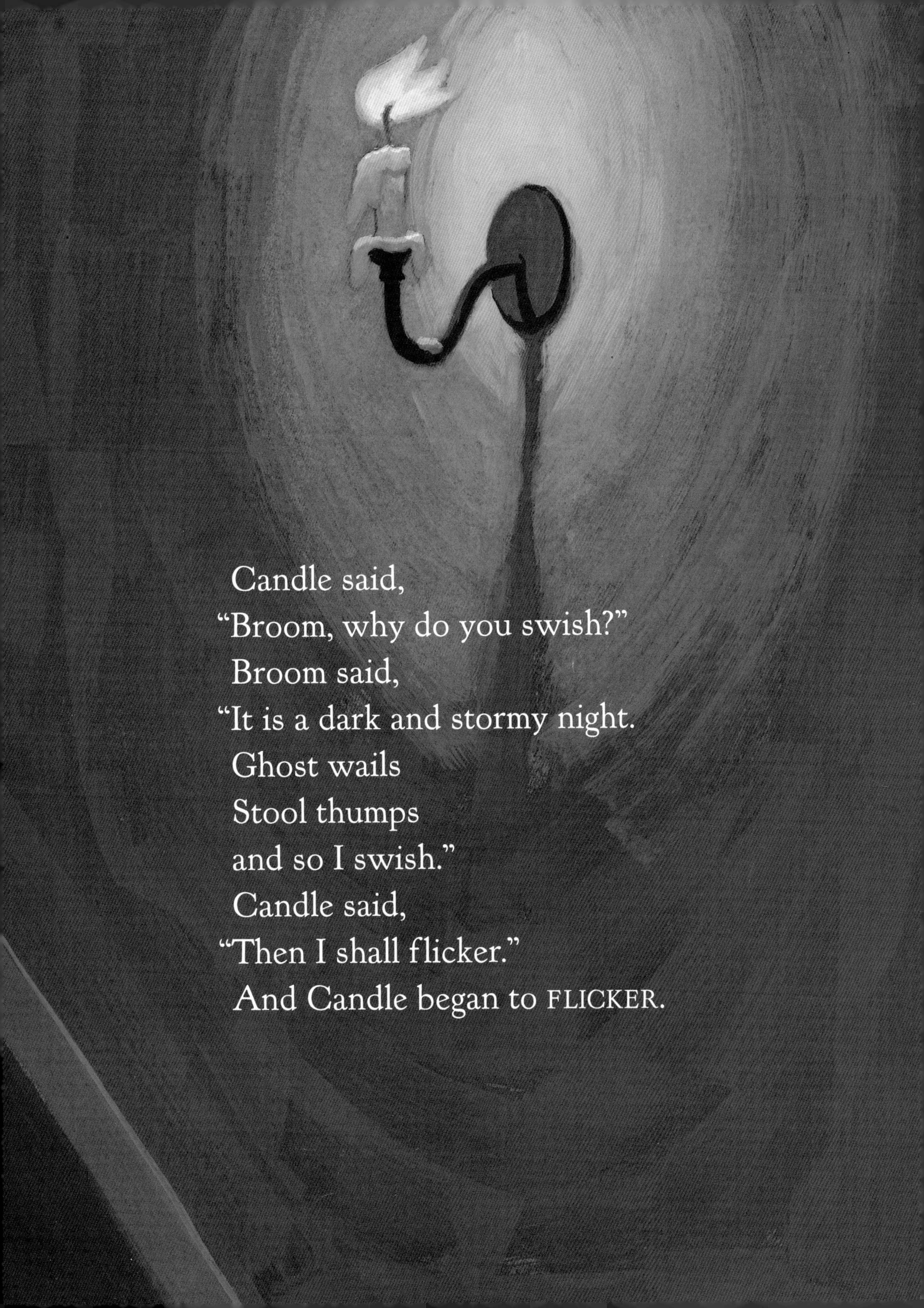

Candle said,
"Broom, why do you swish?"
Broom said,
"It is a dark and stormy night.
Ghost wails
Stool thumps
and so I swish."
Candle said,
"Then I shall flicker."
And Candle began to FLICKER.

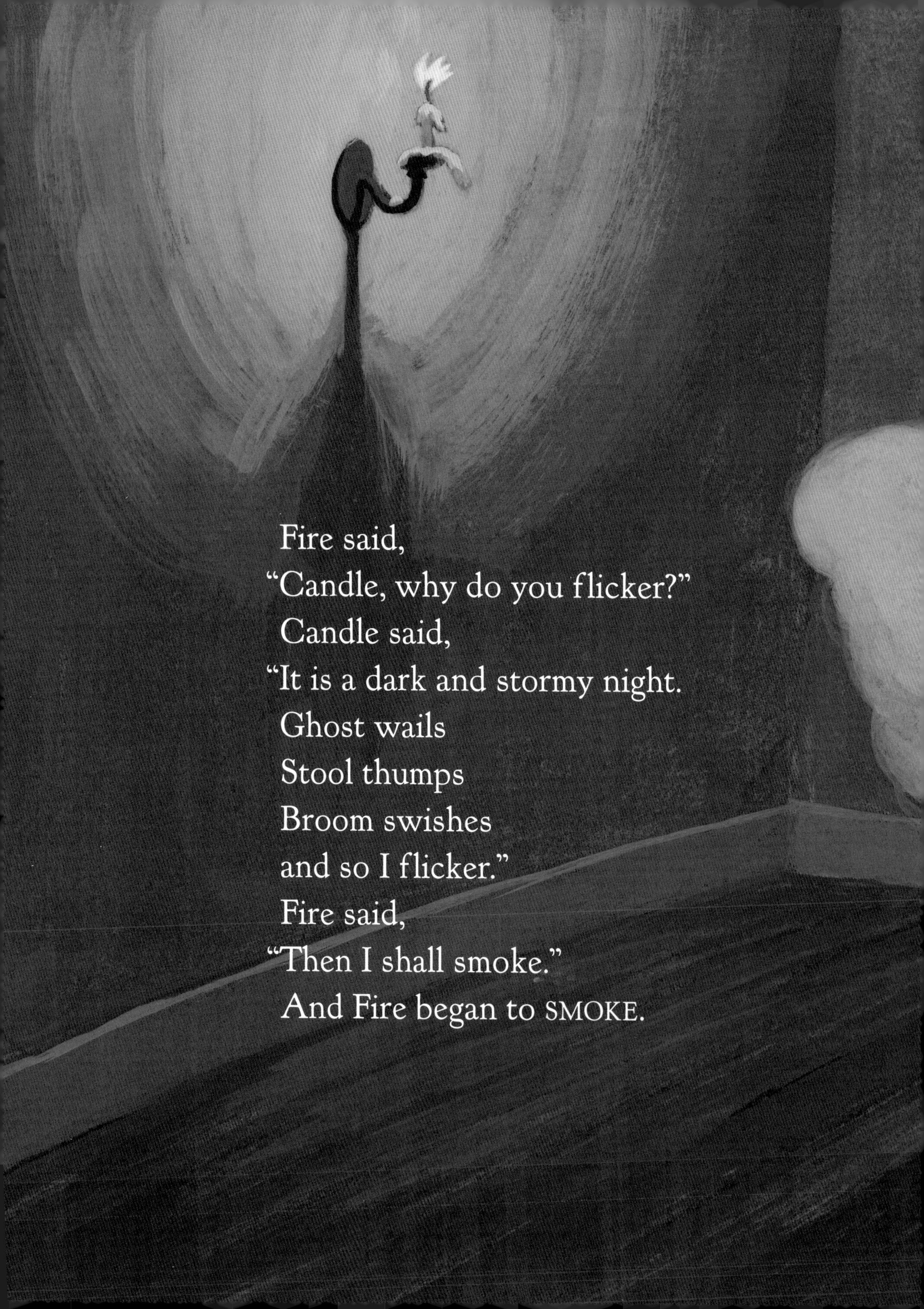

Fire said,
"Candle, why do you flicker?"
Candle said,
"It is a dark and stormy night.
Ghost wails
Stool thumps
Broom swishes
and so I flicker."
Fire said,
"Then I shall smoke."
And Fire began to SMOKE.

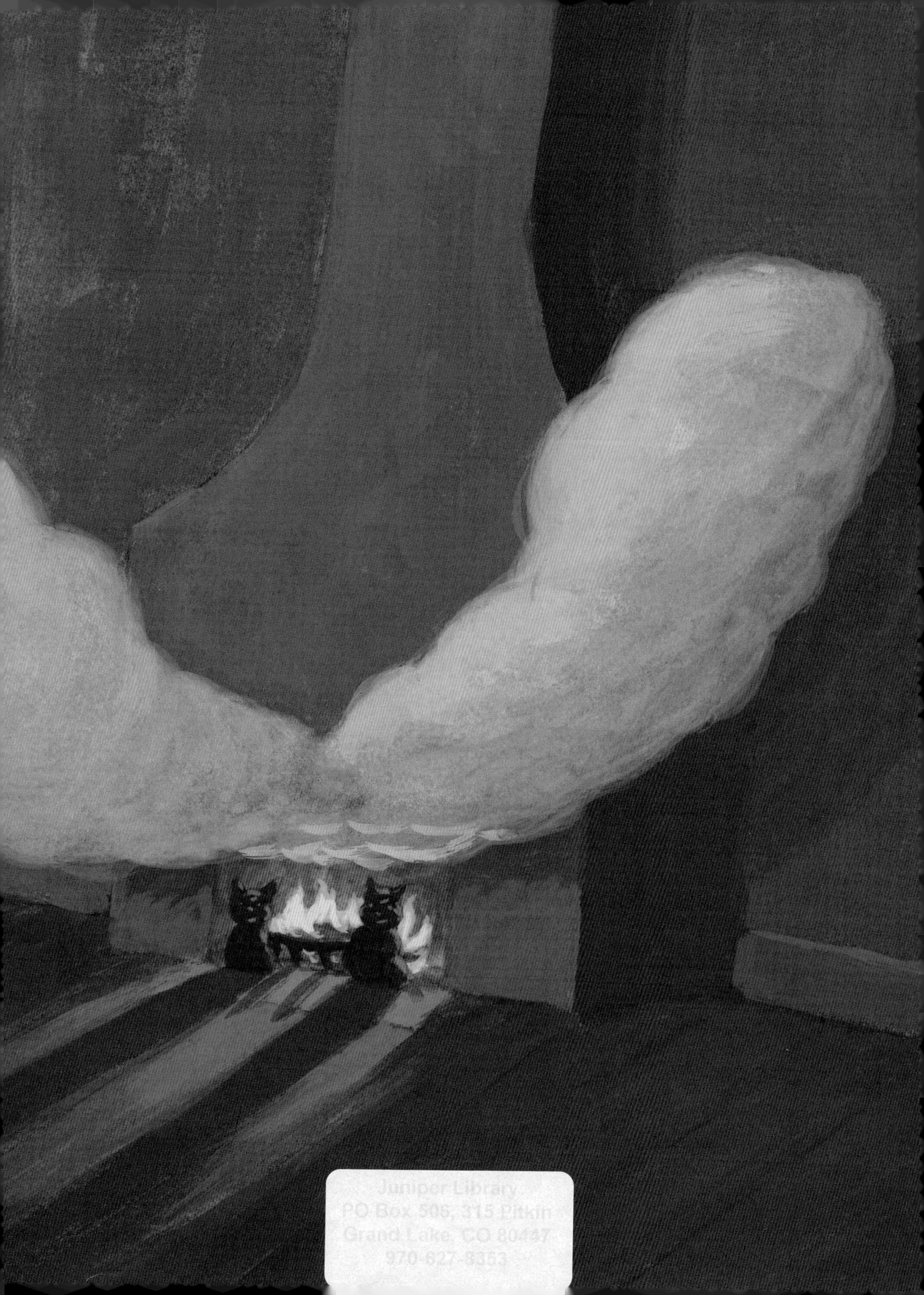

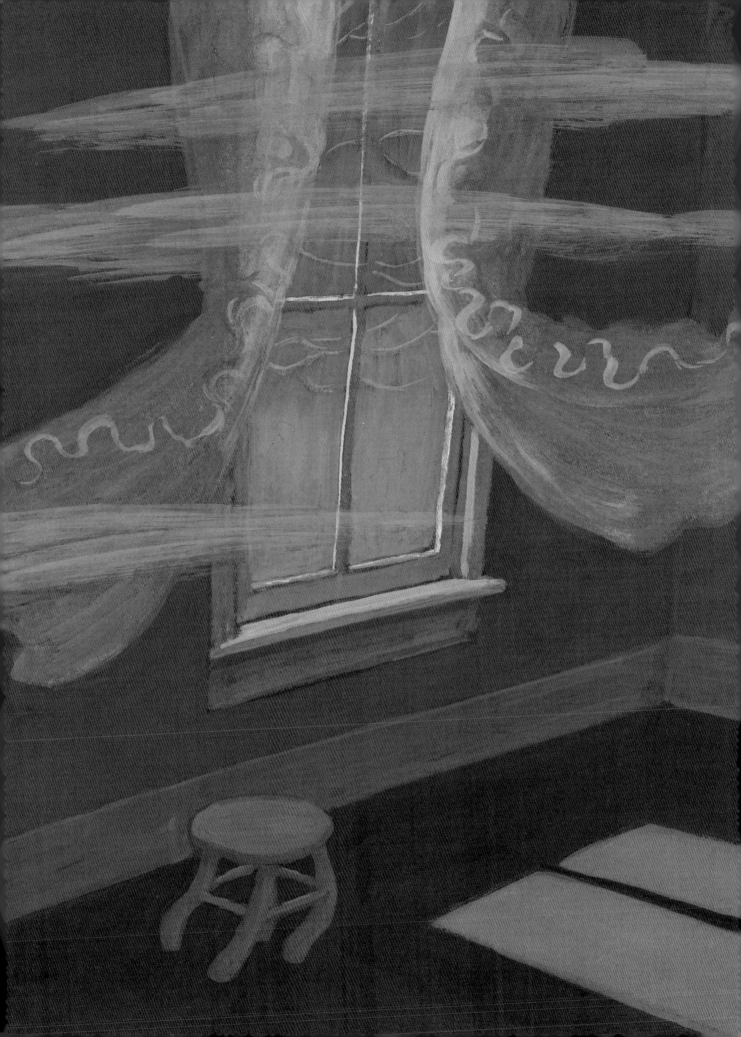

Window said,
"Fire, why do you smoke?"
Fire said,
"It is a dark and stormy night.
Ghost wails
Stool thumps
Broom swishes
Candle flickers
and so I smoke."
Window said,
"Then I shall rattle."
And Window began to RATTLE.

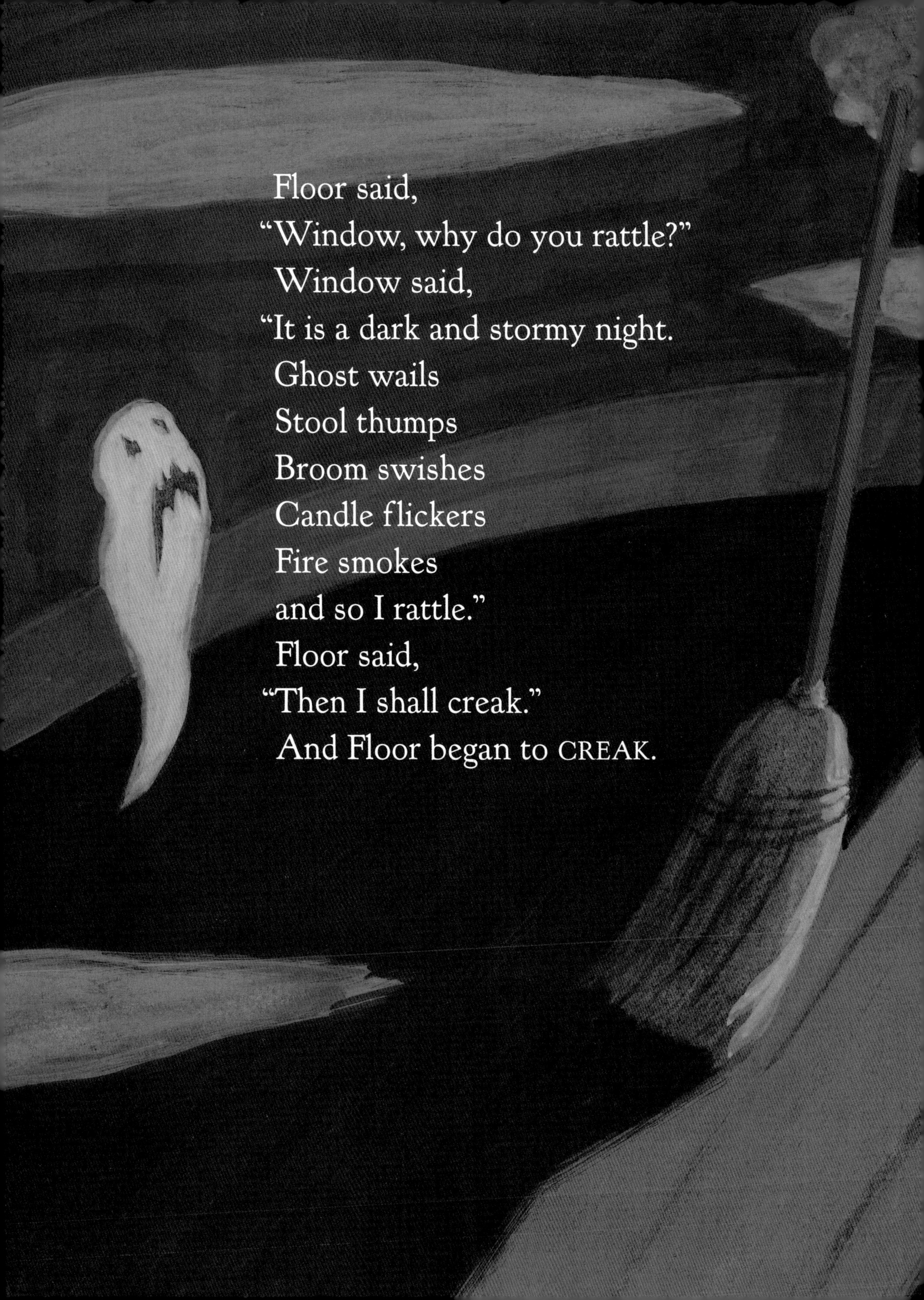

Floor said,
"Window, why do you rattle?"
Window said,
"It is a dark and stormy night.
Ghost wails
Stool thumps
Broom swishes
Candle flickers
Fire smokes
and so I rattle."
Floor said,
"Then I shall creak."
And Floor began to CREAK.

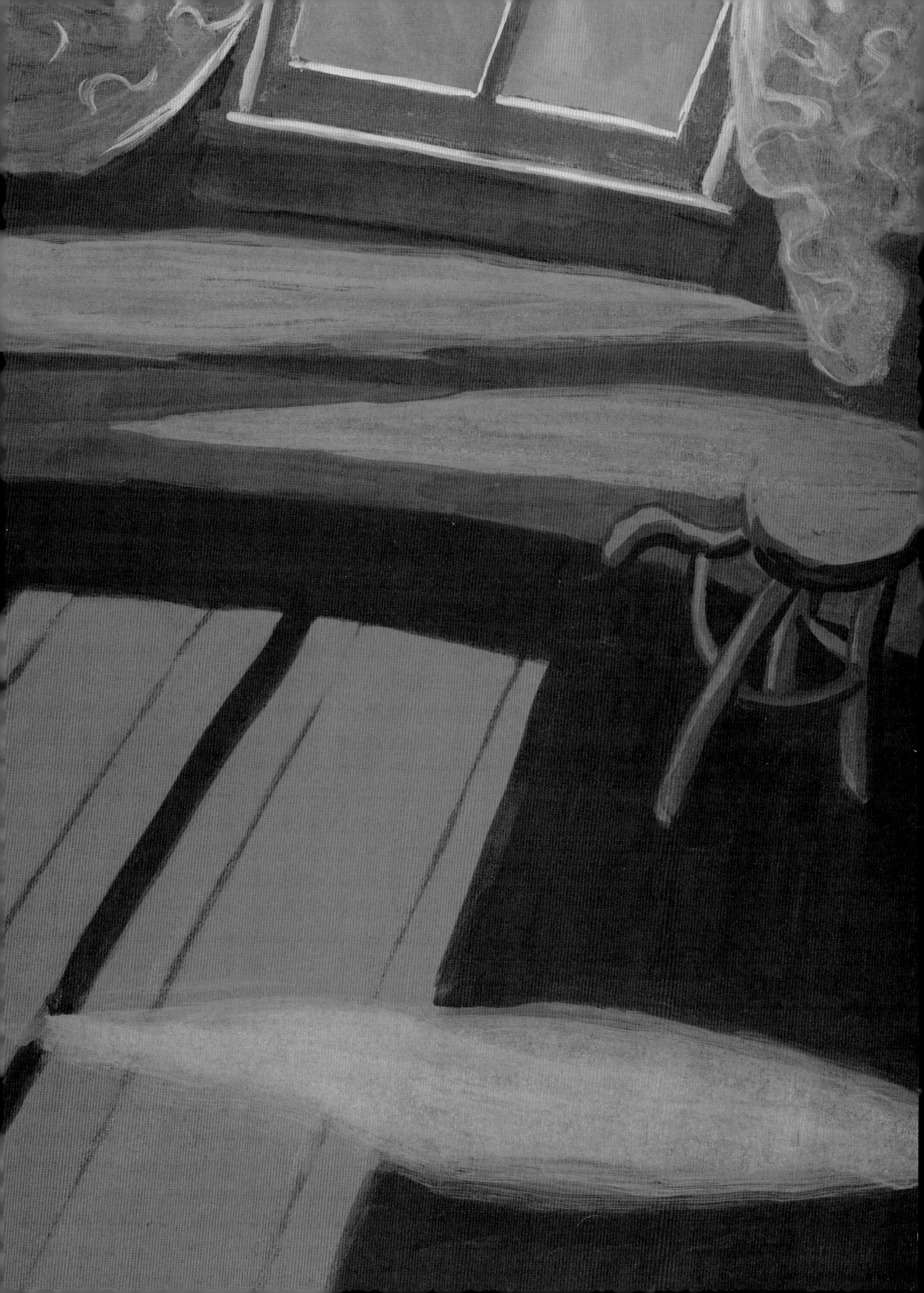

Door said,
"Floor, why do you creak?"
Floor said,
"It is a dark and stormy night.
Ghost wails
Stool thumps
Broom swishes
Candle flickers
Fire smokes
Window rattles
and so I creak."
Door said,
"Then I shall slam."
And Door began to SLAM.

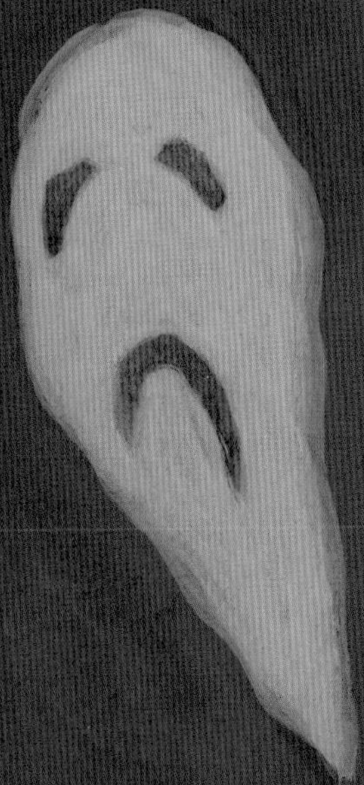

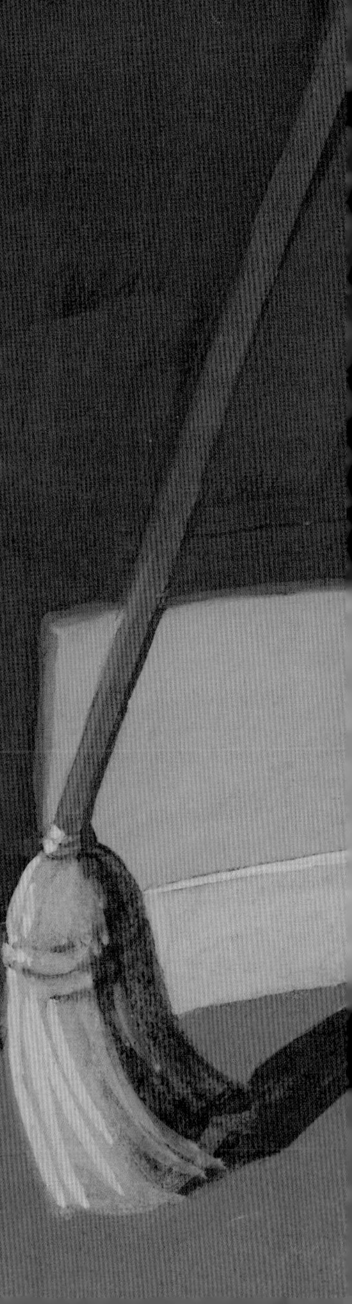

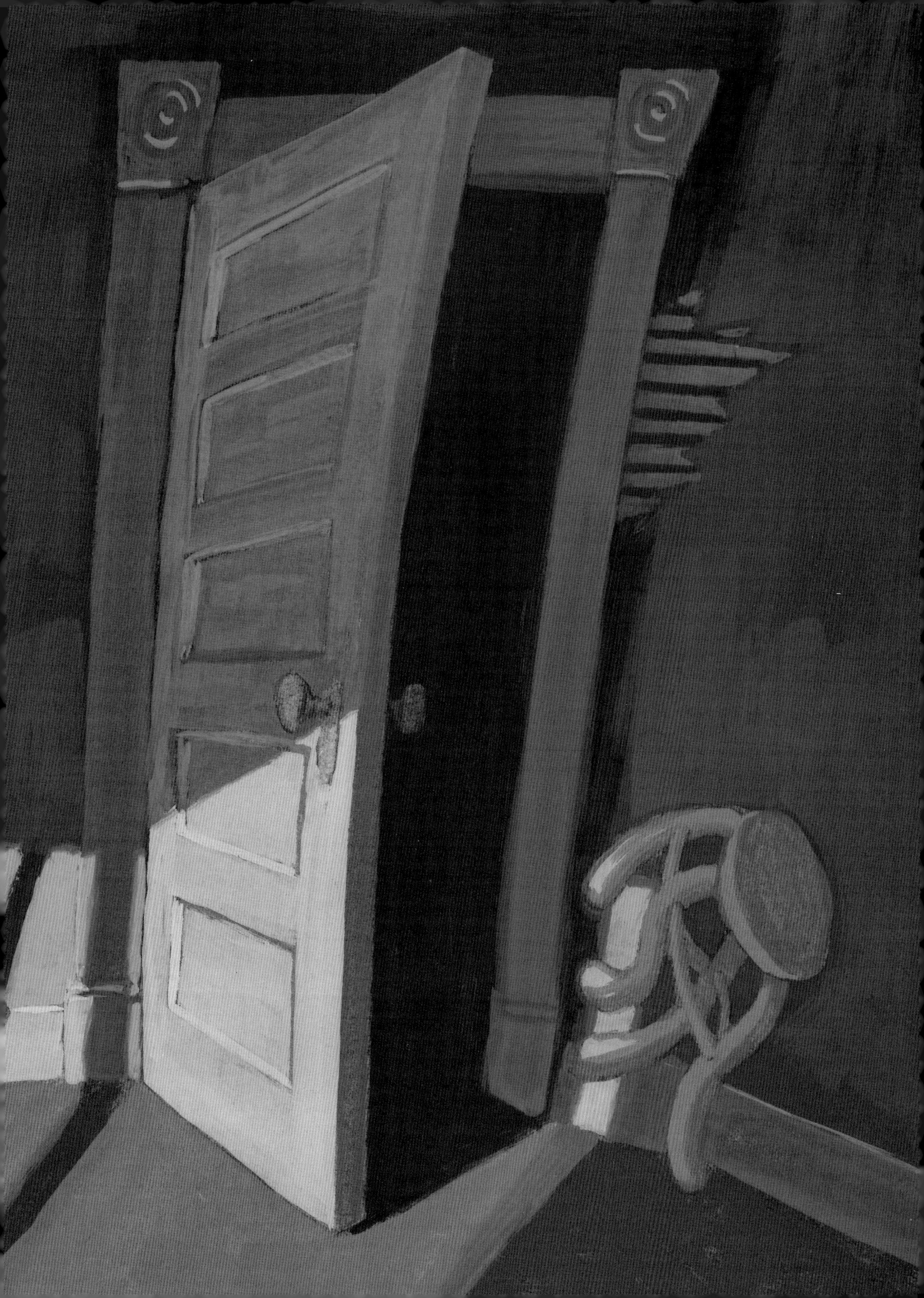

Owl said,
"Door, why do you slam?"
Door said,
"It is a dark and stormy night.
Ghost wails
Stool thumps
Broom swishes
Candle flickers
Fire smokes
Window rattles
Floor creaks
and so I slam."
Owl said,
"Then I shall hoot."
And Owl began to HOOT.

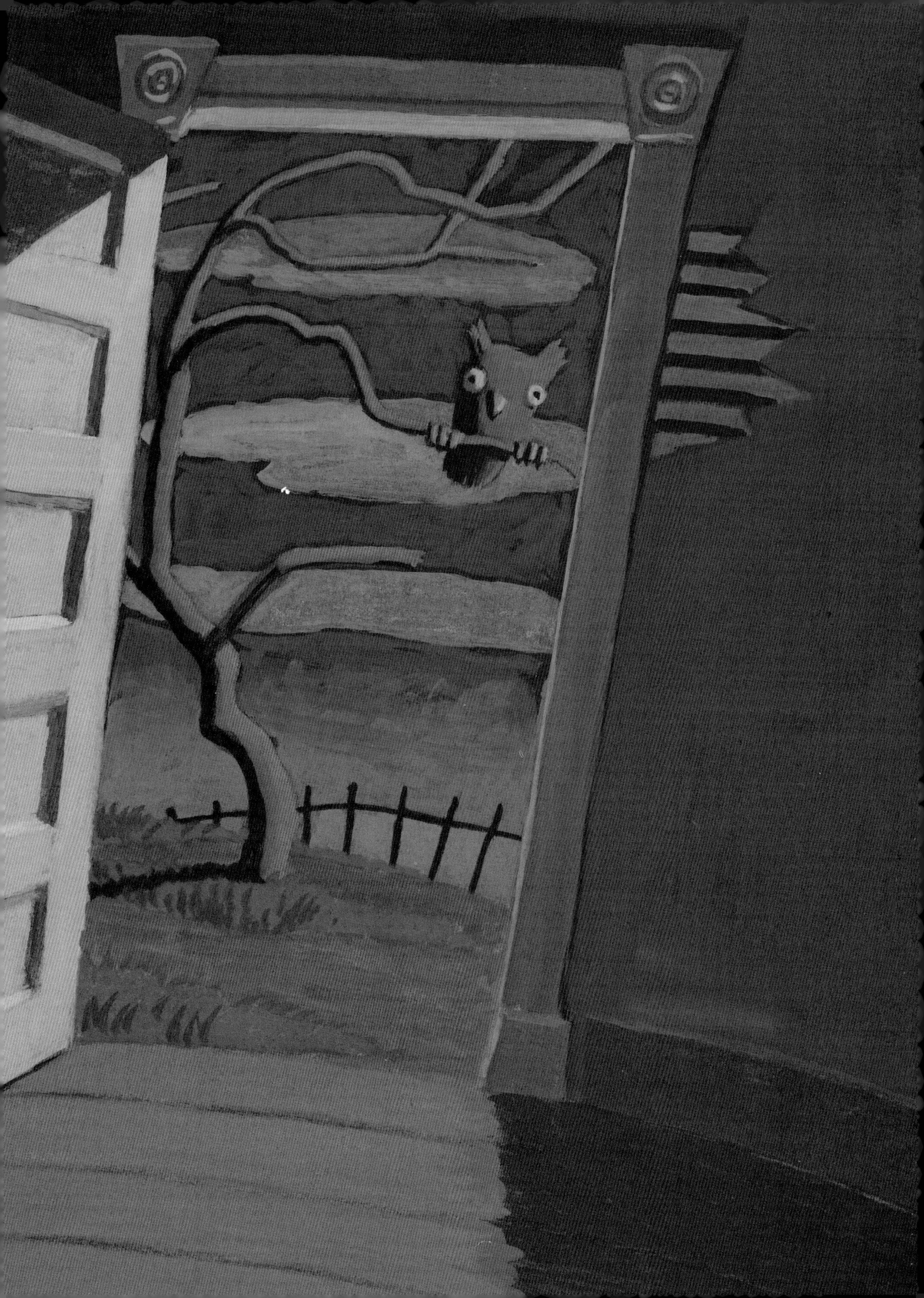

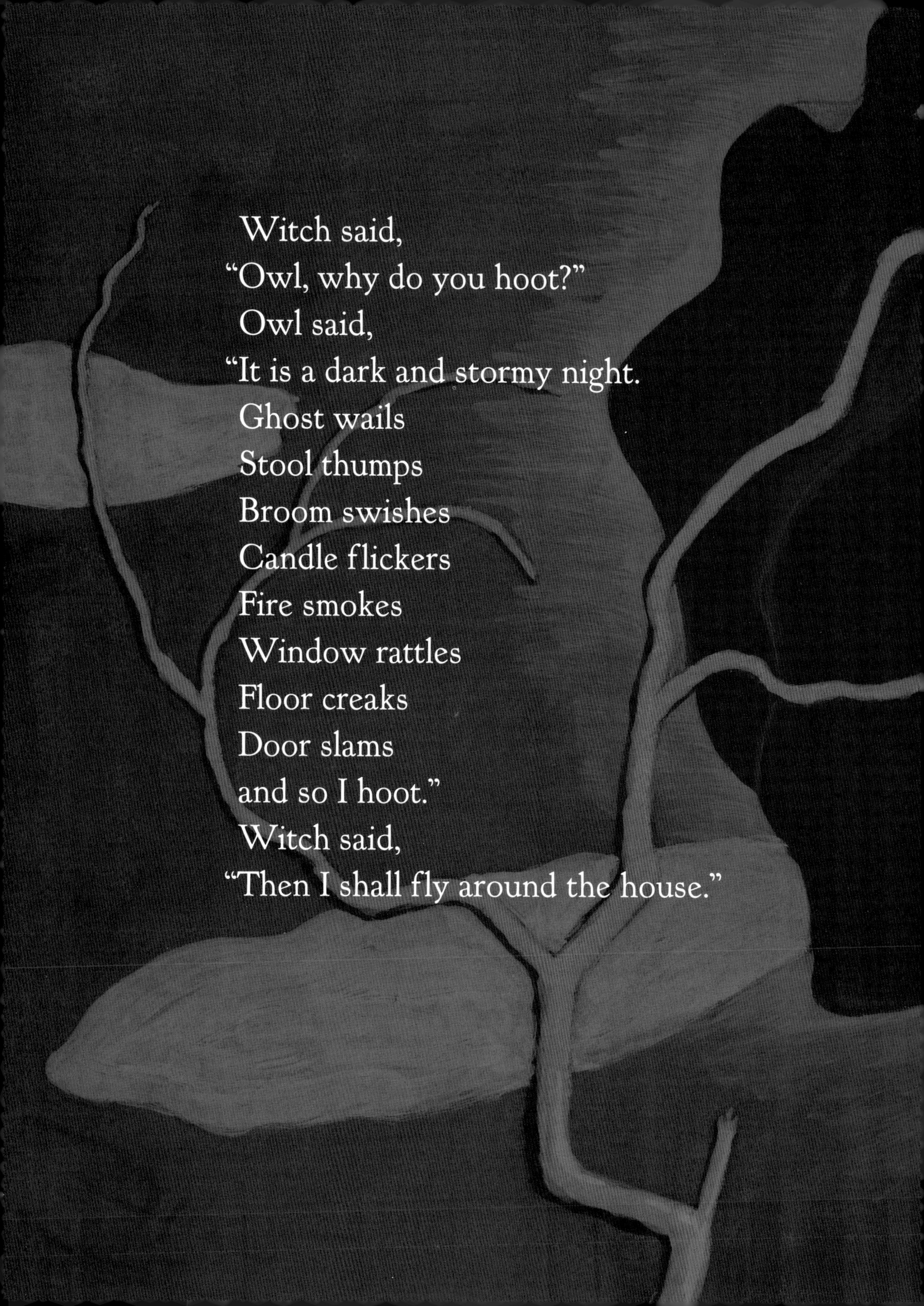

Witch said,
"Owl, why do you hoot?"
Owl said,
"It is a dark and stormy night.
Ghost wails
Stool thumps
Broom swishes
Candle flickers
Fire smokes
Window rattles
Floor creaks
Door slams
and so I hoot."
Witch said,
"Then I shall fly around the house."

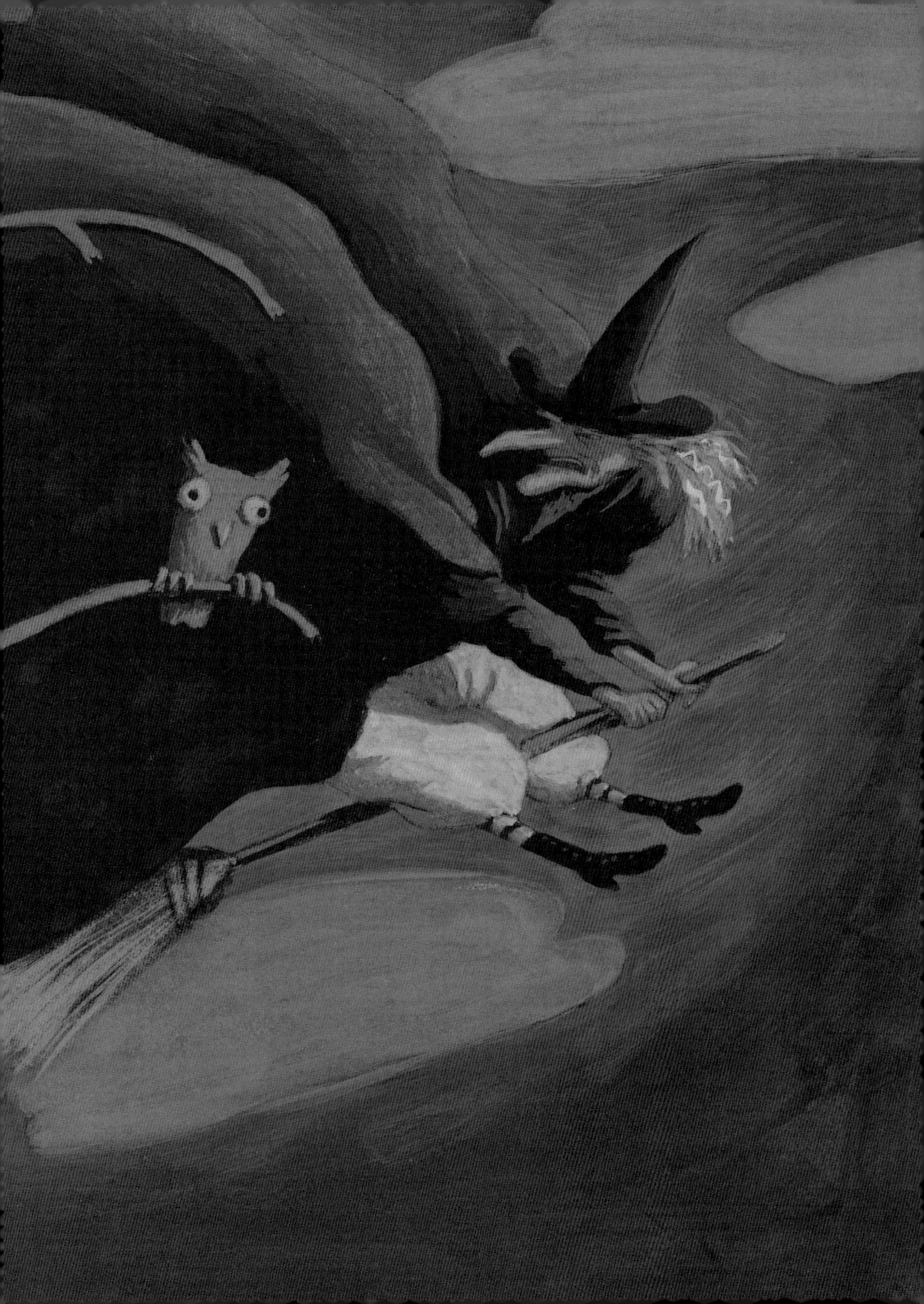

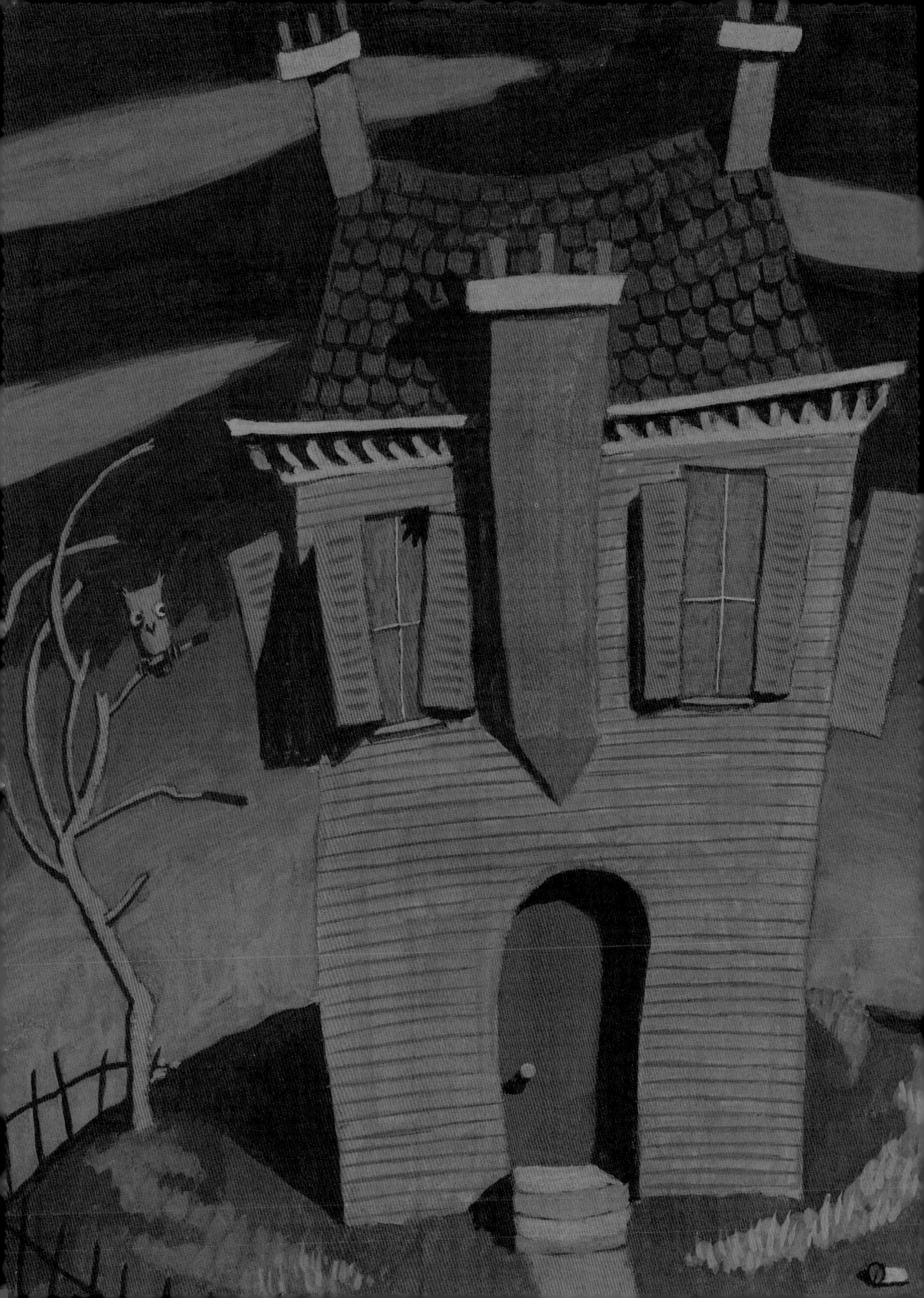

Wind said,
"Witch, why do you fly around the house?"
Witch said,
"It is a dark and stormy night.
Ghost wails
Stool thumps
Broom swishes
Candle flickers
Fire smokes
Window rattles
Floor creaks
Door slams
Owl hoots
and so I fly around the house."
Wind said,
"Then I shall BLOW."

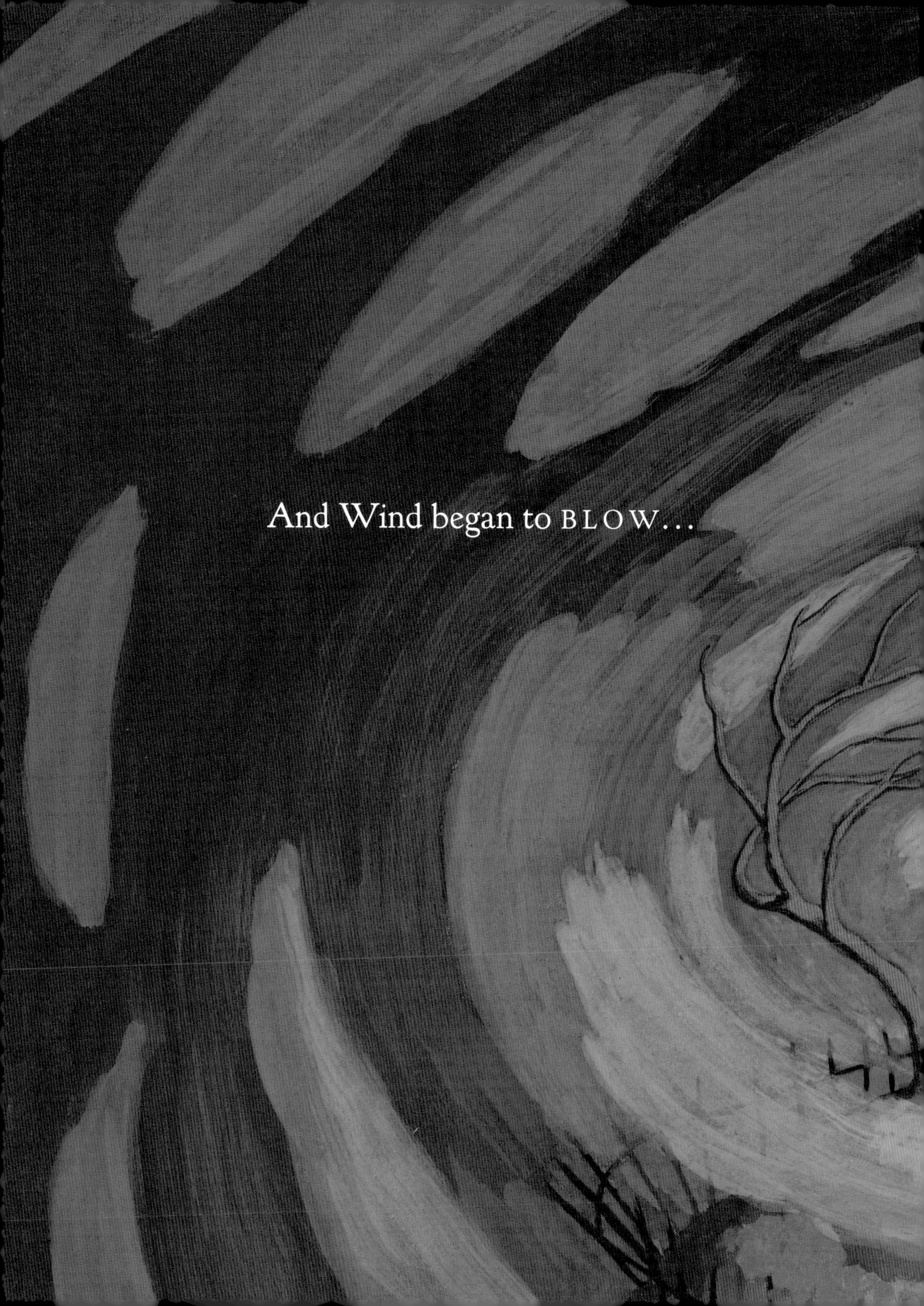

And Wind began to BLOW...

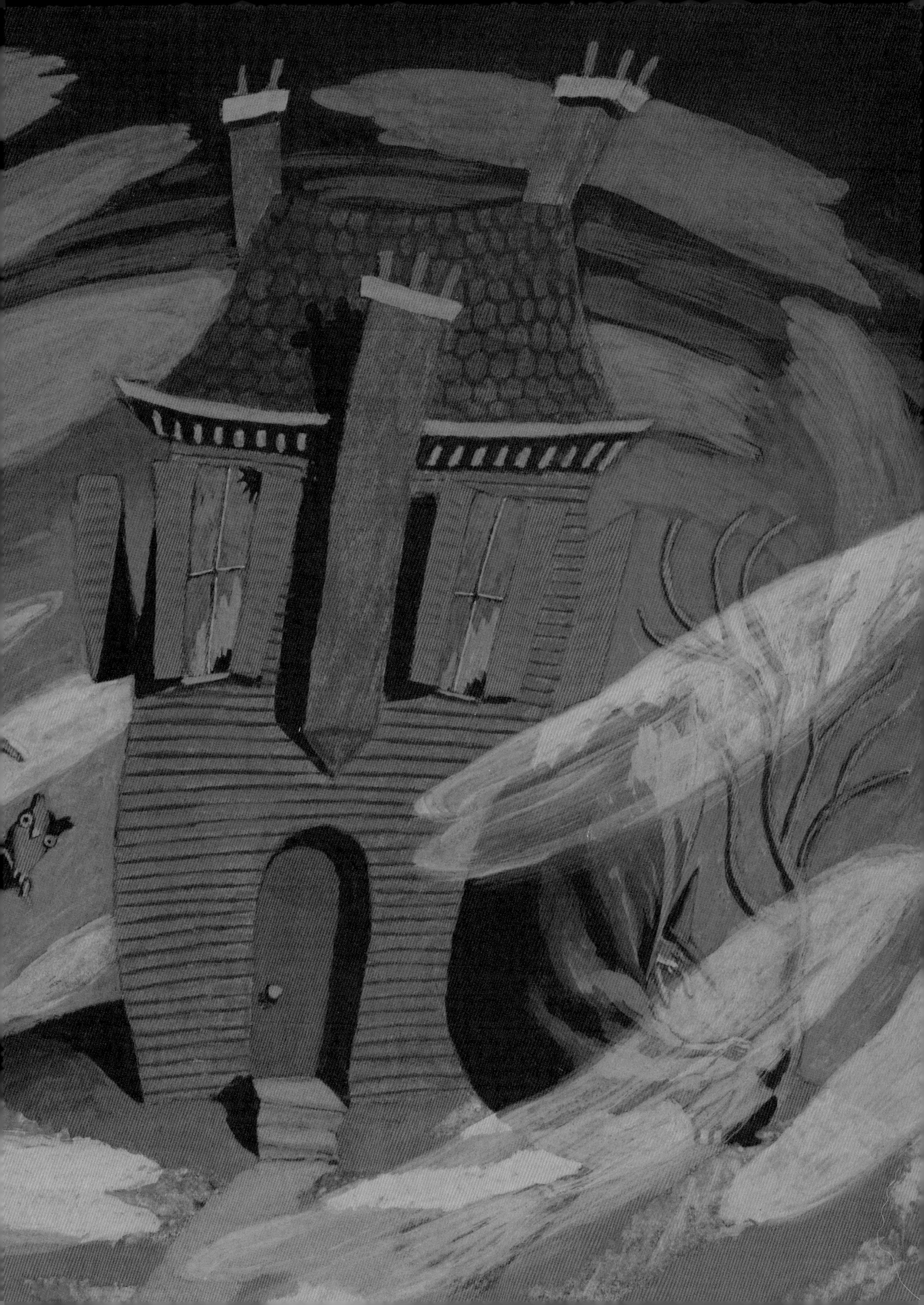

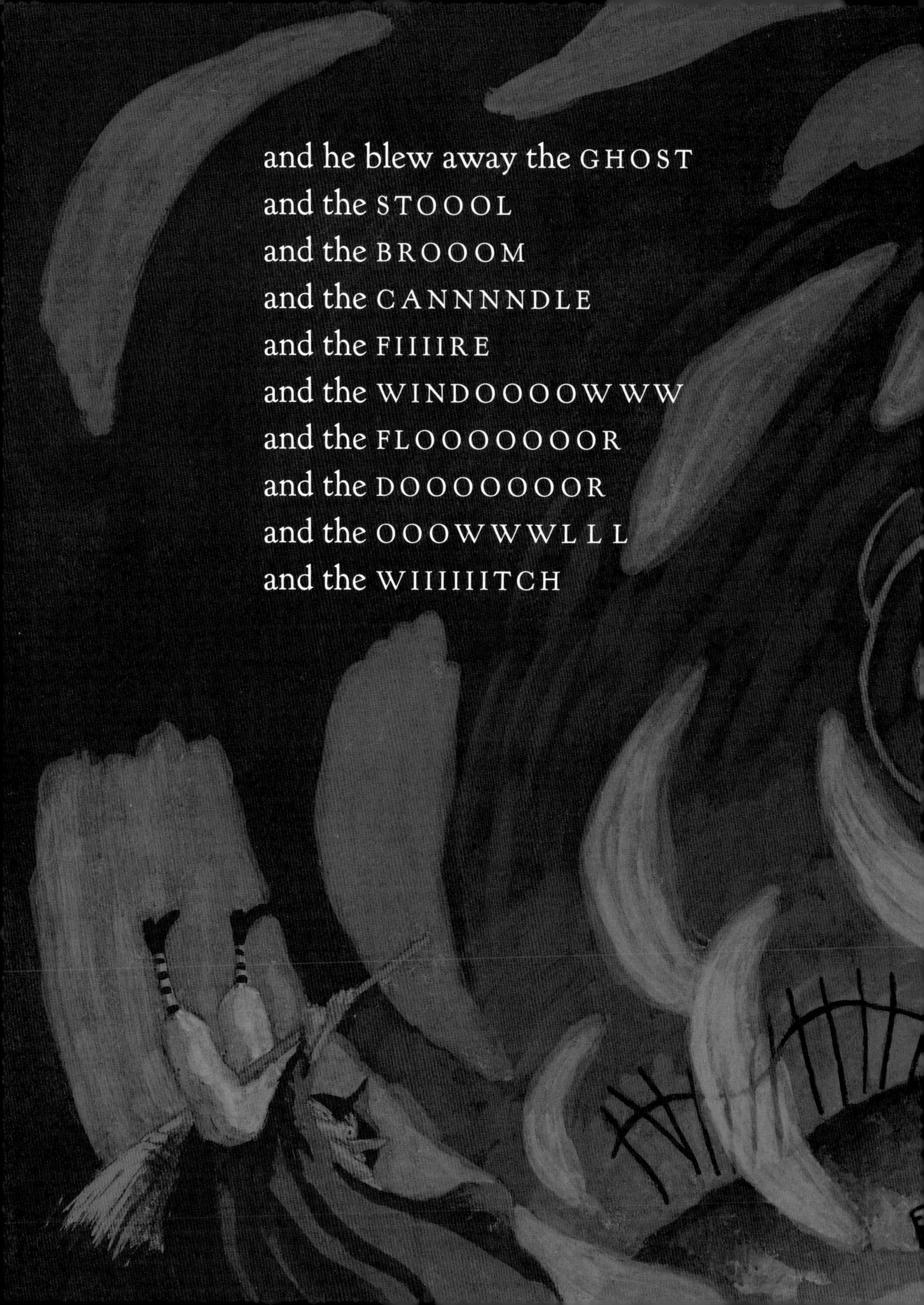

and he blew away the GHOST
and the STOOOL
and the BROOOM
and the CANNNNDLE
and the FIIIIRE
and the WINDOOOOWWW
and the FLOOOOOOOR
and the DOOOOOOOR
and the OOOWWWLLL
and the WIIIIIITCH

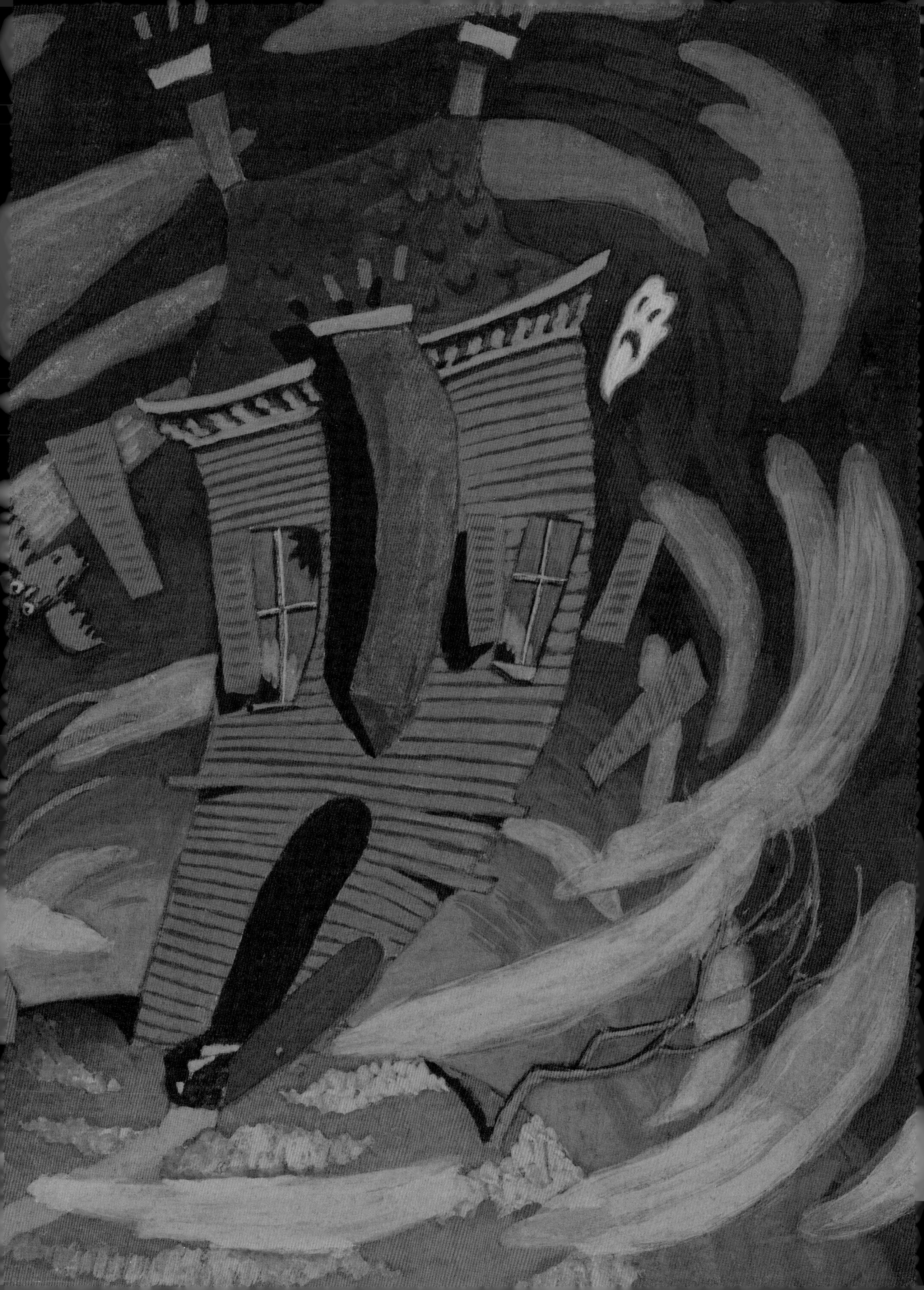

and they didn't come back
till HALLOWEEN NIGHT!

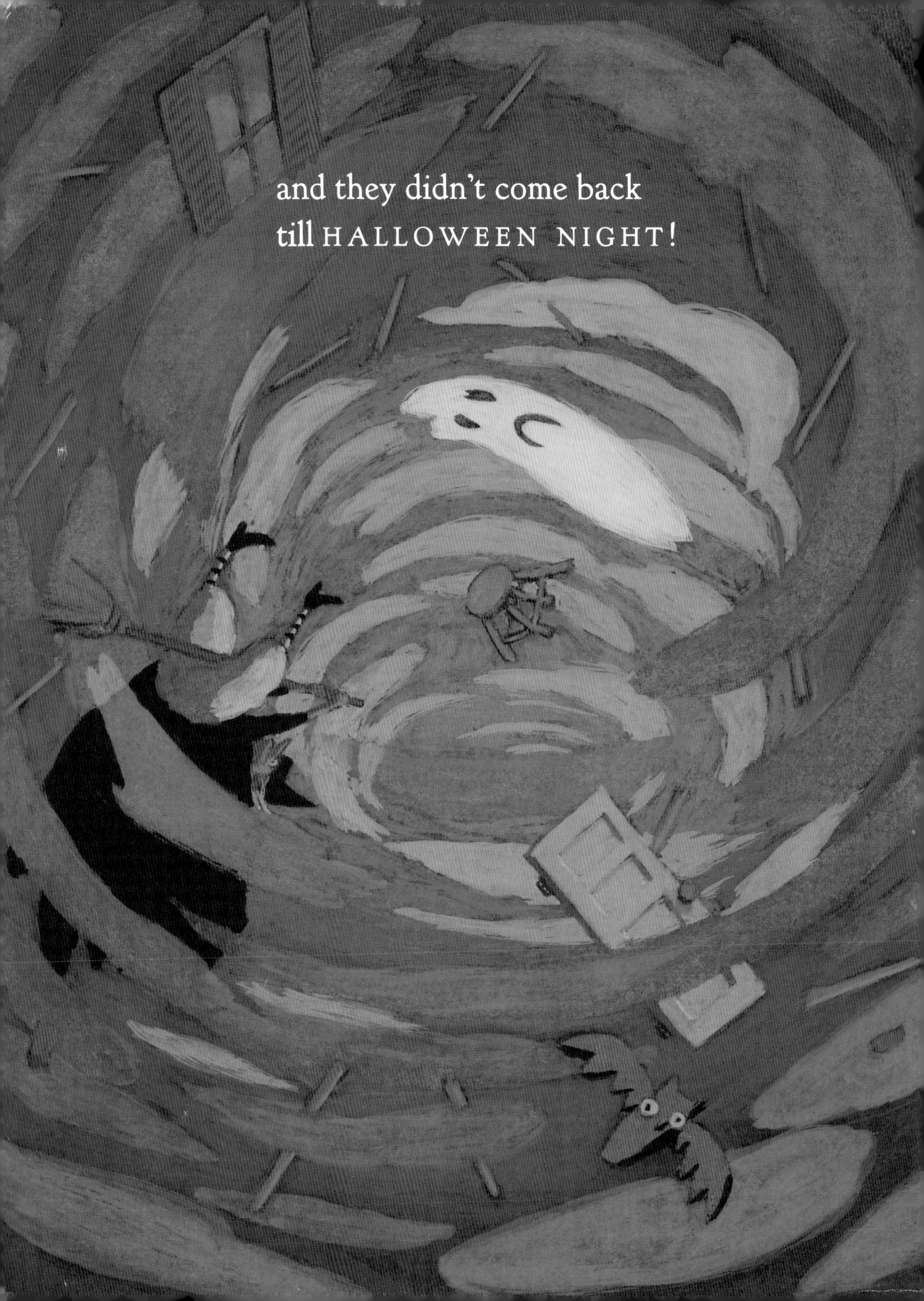